# MONSTER HUNTERS
## track the turtle lake monster

by Jan Fields
Illustrated by Scott Brundage

Calico

An Imprint of Magic Wagon
abdopublishing.com

**abdopublishing.com**

Published by Magic Wagon, a division of ABDO, PO Box 398166, Minneapolis, Minnesota 55439. Copyright © 2017 by Abdo Consulting Group, Inc. International copyrights reserved in all countries. No part of this book may be reproduced in any form without written permission from the publisher. Calico™ is a trademark and logo of Magic Wagon.

Printed in the United States of America, North Mankato, Minnesota.
052016
092016

Written by Jan Fields
Illustrated by Scott Brundage
Edited by Tamara L. Britton & Megan M. Gunderson
Design Contributors: Candice Keimig & Laura Mitchell

## Library of Congress Cataloging-in-Publication Data

Names: Fields, Jan, author. | Brundage, Scott, illustrator.
Title: Track the Turtle Lake monster / by Jan Fields ; illustrated by Scott
  Brundage.
Description: Minneapolis, MN : Magic Wagon, [2017] | Series: Monster
hunters
  | Summary: The Discover Cryptids filming crew heads to Canada to
  investigate the Turtle Lake monster which is apparently sinking boats--but
  when the lake front diner burns down, they begin to think that this
  monster may be a lot more human than cryptid.
Identifiers: LCCN 2016002311 (print) | LCCN 2016005460 (ebook) | ISBN
  9781624021558 (lib. bdg.) | ISBN 9781680779851 (ebook)
Subjects: LCSH: Monsters--Juvenile fiction. | Curiosities and
  wonders--Juvenile fiction. | Action photography--Juvenile fiction. |
  Conspiracies--Juvenile fiction. | Adventure stories. |
  Saskatchewan--Juvenile fiction. | CYAC: Mystery and detective stories. |
  Adventure and adventurers--Fiction. | Monsters--Fiction. | Curiosities and
  wonders--Fiction. | Photography--Fiction. | Conspiracies--Fiction. |
  Saskatchewan--Fiction. | Canada--Fiction. | GSAFD: Adventure fiction. |
  Mystery fiction.
Classification: LCC PZ7.F479177 Tp 2016 (print) | LCC PZ7.F479177 (ebook)
  DDC 813.6--dc23
LC record available at http://lccn.loc.gov/2016002311

# TABLE of CONTENTS

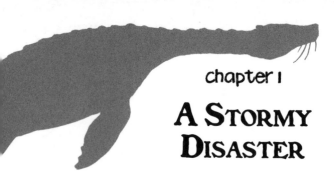

## chapter 1

# A STORMY DISASTER

Rain slammed into the window beside Gabe. The van wallowed through another deep puddle, sending Tyler tumbling from the seat beside him. Gabe grabbed his best friend's arm and hauled him back upright.

"Michigan sure is rainy," Gabe said.

"We're going to die," Tyler wailed.

"Just hang on," Ben yelled back as he wrestled the van's steering wheel. "If we can get to the top of this ridge, I think we'll be above the floodwater."

Gabe hugged his backpack tighter. It held the camera they used to film the *Discover Cryptids* web episodes, and a few survival supplies.

Sean leaned over the seat from behind. "The

rising floodwater may force the Waheela to head for higher ground as well. That will mean we have less area to search."

"So when we do get ahead of the flood," Tyler said, "we'll probably be eaten by a bear-wolf monster."

"The legends say the Waheela doesn't eat people," Sean said.

Tyler huffed in relief. "That's good."

"It just bites their heads off."

"What?"

Pulling his backpack closer, Gabe leaned forward to stare through the front windshield.

The van worked its way around a curve, revealing water rushing across the road. Ben slammed on the brakes, but the van barely slowed as it slipped on the muddy road. Instead it lumbered into the water like a hippo in a nature documentary and stopped. For a moment, the tires spun. Then the motor quit.

"Ben!" Gabe shouted.

"The water's too deep. Nothing I can do." He unfastened his seat belt and turned around rapidly. "We're going to have to have a go at it on foot. Tyler, grab some rope and put it in your backpack. Can anyone get a phone signal here?"

After some fumbling, everyone reported the same thing. No cell service.

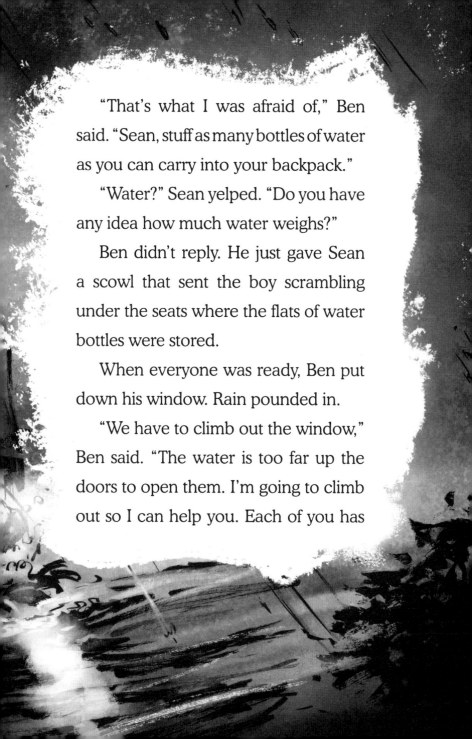

"That's what I was afraid of," Ben said. "Sean, stuff as many bottles of water as you can carry into your backpack."

"Water?" Sean yelped. "Do you have any idea how much water weighs?"

Ben didn't reply. He just gave Sean a scowl that sent the boy scrambling under the seats where the flats of water bottles were stored.

When everyone was ready, Ben put down his window. Rain pounded in.

"We have to climb out the window," Ben said. "The water is too far up the doors to open them. I'm going to climb out so I can help you. Each of you has to follow. Climb out onto the roof, then carefully onto the hood. You should be able to jump past the water from the hood." He turned to look directly at Gabe. "Give me a minute to get outside, then you climb out. You probably won't be able to see me, but I'll get you."

"Okay," Gabe said. He watched his brother wriggle out the window. He knew it would be easier for him. He was so much smaller.

Gabe waited a moment after Ben was gone, then scrambled into the front seat and stuck his left arm and head out the window. Cold rain drenched his hair in seconds and stung his eyes. He rubbed his eyes on his shoulder, trying to clear his vision.

A hand grabbed his wrist. Ben's voice called from above, "I got you! Climb on out."

As Gabe scrambled through the window, Ben caught his other hand and hauled him onto the van roof. Ben half shouted in his ear, "I'll

lower you to the hood. Be careful, it slopes. You'll need to jump from the hood to clear the water, but throw your backpack first so it doesn't weigh you down."

"How far is the jump?" Gabe asked nervously.

Ben didn't exactly answer. He patted his brother on the arm. "You can do it. Go. I have to help the others."

Ben lowered Gabe to the hood, then let go. Gabe had never felt as alone in his life as he did while standing in the pounding rain on the slippery hood. He carefully edged out farther onto it. Though it was only early evening, the pounding rain made it much darker. Gabe wiped his arm across his eyes, then squinted, trying to see the edge of the rushing water.

Something big and shadowy moved in the darkness beyond. Gabe gasped, sucking in enough rainwater to make him cough. Whatever moved in the shadows slipped farther away, out

of Gabe's line of sight. He heard a sound, like a barking shout. With the roar of the pounding rain, he couldn't identify it.

Suddenly Sean's calm remarks that the Waheela would be out looking for higher ground came back to him. Somewhere out there in the darkness, a Waheela lurked, maybe. And maybe the legendary bear-wolf creature that bit off people's heads was exactly what moved through the shadows in the spot Ben wanted him to jump.

"Gabe!" Ben bellowed. "You need to jump so I can lower Tyler down to the hood!"

Gabe considered telling Ben about the movement in the shadows. But what could his brother do? They were trapped, and the floodwater was rising. He really had no choice.

Gabe shucked out of his backpack and heaved it as hard as he could, directly toward the spot he'd seen something move. Nothing

yelped or growled. But would he even hear the Waheela over the sound of the rain?

"Jump, Gabe, jump!" Ben bellowed.

Gabe took a deep breath, tensed his muscles, and jumped, flying into the darkness. He didn't land on the hard ground as he expected. He didn't even land in water. Instead, he hit something that grunted. Gabe's numb fingers sunk into wet, tangled hair of some kind. Gabe screamed.

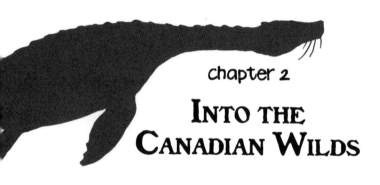

## chapter 2

# INTO THE CANADIAN WILDS

Tyler leaned over the seat of the van, looking between Gabe and Sean. "Why does Canada look so much like all the other places we go to look for cryptids?"

"Cryptids are creatures of myth and legend that may exist," Sean lectured, "but no one has yet found proof. Logically, they're going to be in wild areas. Cryptids don't hang out at the mall."

"But they do hang out in the United States," Tyler said. "So why are we in Canada?"

"Waheelas are more common in Canada than in Michigan. I thought we'd have better luck hunting one up here," Ben said.

"I vote that we never look for Waheelas again," Tyler said. "We almost died."

"That's a little dramatic," Ben said.

Gabe shivered as he remembered his jump into the darkness. Thankfully he'd landed on a big, bearded hunter who wasn't all that mad about having a kid fly out of the darkness and slam into him. The hunter had even used the winch on his truck to pull the van out of the floodwater.

Ben had told the man about the cryptids they'd hunted. He insisted that if they really wanted to see some scary monsters, they should go to Canada. So they went.

"This may be even more interesting than the Waheela," Ben said. "We are looking for a creature that seems to be waging war on the local population."

"Waging war?" Tyler yelped. "You mean eating people?"

Ben laughed. "No people snacks so far. Just a few rough bumps."

"Rough bumps?" Tyler echoed.

"Sean," Ben said, "how about you tell us some cool stuff about Saskatchewan?"

Sean perked up beside Gabe. Tyler groaned and slumped in his seat, muttering, "You could have just asked me to stop talking."

Sean ignored Tyler and slipped into his fun facts voice. "Half of the land in Saskatchewan, Canada, is forest."

"I can believe that," Gabe said, looking out the window. Both sides of the road were thickly wooded. He saw dark evergreens and pale, slender birch trees. Through the trees, he glimpsed narrow roads or trails that vanished as they sped past. A pond caught the light, winking at them like a small jewel. Then they were past that as well.

"There are over one hundred thousand lakes, rivers, and streams."

"Sounds soggy," Tyler said.

"Not really," Sean said. "Saskatchewan is known for its hot, dry summers and almost constant windy conditions. In fact, the weather has been especially dry this year."

*At least we can skip nearly drowning in a flood,* Gabe thought.

"Hey, do you have a fun fact about the closest place to eat?" Tyler asked. "I'm starving."

"You're always starving," Ben said. "We aren't far from Turtle Lake. The rental agent said there's a small grocery store and diner near our cabin. We can eat there."

"If I survive," Tyler moaned.

They drove until the lake appeared through the trees. Tyler continued groaning and predicting his near death. Finally, Ben said, "That must be the grocery and diner."

Tyler waved his hands in the air. "I'm saved!"

"Who wants to unload our stuff before we eat?" Ben asked.

No one.

Ben laughed and pulled into the gravel parking lot next to a long log cabin with a narrow front porch that ran the length of the building. As soon as the engine stopped, the boys were out of their seat belts.

"You guys go in," Ben said. "I'm going to call the real estate agent and make sure I know the way to our cabin from here."

"Be sure it has Wi-Fi," Sean insisted. "I'll need it for research."

Tyler hauled the van's door open. "I'll be happy if the cabin doesn't have spiders."

Sean followed Tyler out the door. "Spiders are an important part of the ecosystem."

Gabe sighed as the argument washed over him. He shoved his hands into his pockets and trotted ahead to the diner. A woman at the door looked them over. "You boys need to wait on your parents?"

Gabe shook his head. "We can sit. My brother will be here in a minute. He'll find us."

She handed them each a menu. "Sit anywhere. You missed the lunch rush, and it's too early for the supper stampede, so there are plenty of choices."

A teenager wiping tables nearby spoke up. "Mom, the last time you had a crowd, I wasn't born yet."

"Oh, hush, you!" The woman shook her finger at the teen, though she was smiling as she did it.

Gabe chose a table near a window so he could watch for Ben. Tyler didn't even glance out the window. He started reading from the one-page menu. "Hamburger soup? Who makes soup from hamburger?"

"The same people who make burgers from bison," Sean answered, reaching across to point at a spot lower on the menu.

Tyler wrinkled his nose. "Don't they have anything normal? And what is poutine?"

Sean immediately snapped back into fun facts mode. "Poutine is a popular Canadian dish. It originated in Quebec. There are many variations, but the classic poutine is French fries with cheese curds on top, covered in gravy."

Tyler looked at Sean suspiciously. "Really?

Sean nodded.

"Sounds a little weird," Tyler said. "But at least I know I like all the ingredients. I'll try that."

Sean peered closer at the menu. "Maybe I'll have the venison lasagna."

"Venison?" Tyler said.

"Deer."

"Deer! Is there anything Canadians won't eat?" Tyler asked.

"We try to draw the line at kids. We hardly ever eat them. Well, sometimes with a really good gravy."

## chapter 3

# THE TURTLE LAKE TALES

The boys turned to face a big man with sparkling eyes who raised his coffee cup to them and smiled. "So where are your parents?"

"In the United States," Sean said.

"But my brother is out in the van," Gabe said. "He'll be in here in a minute."

"If this isn't a family trip, what has brought you up to Saskatchewan?"

"We're looking for the Turtle Lake Monster," Sean said.

The man raised both eyebrows. "Well, then I take back what I said about eating kids. The lake monster might just take a bite or two."

"Don't be scaring these boys!" The woman who had met them at the door stood near their

table. She held an order pad and shook her pen at the seated man. "The Turtle Lake Monster doesn't hurt anyone."

"That monster has turned mean and you know it," the man insisted.

"You both believe in the monster?" Gabe said, surprised. "Have you seen it?"

"Not exactly," the woman said. "I was in a boat once when the monster thumped it. We thought it was probably a log at first, but then we didn't see anything. It was the monster being neighborly."

"The creature has been a little *too* neighborly lately," the man said.

"One theory I've read is that the Turtle Lake Monster is an unusually large sturgeon," Sean said. "Do sturgeons bump boats?"

The man nodded his head. "It's certainly possible. But this is not a sturgeon. Netting surveys haven't come up with any sturgeons.

And the commercial fishermen on the lake haven't caught any either."

"What bumped my husband's boat was not a sturgeon," the woman insisted, crossing her arms over her chest and tapping the pen against her forearm. "It was the monster."

Sean crossed his arms. "It's a valid theory. Sturgeons are bottom-feeders so would be rarely spotted. They'd be lurking in the shadows."

The woman shook her head. "The Turtle Lake Monster is big with a scaly head that resembles a dog or maybe a horse. I've had customers who saw the thing poke its head above the water."

Sean said, "I've read the reports."

The woman finally shrugged and said, "How about I take orders instead of arguing?"

"Poutine!" Tyler shouted. "And I want dessert, too. What's good?"

"We have fresh saskatoon berry pie," she said.

"Saskatoon berries?" Tyler repeated, suspicious. "That's not secretly something horrible is it?"

The woman laughed. "Saskatoon berries look like blueberries and taste like magic. You'll love it. Trust me."

Tyler agreed and everyone else added their orders. Just after that, Gabe spotted Ben across the diner. Gabe waved, and his brother quickly strode over to them.

"Cabin's not far," Ben said. "We can walk over after we eat, then see if there's anything we might need to pick up at the grocery here."

"When do we begin our search for the monster?" Sean asked.

"Maybe today. The cabin has a private dock with a boat available," Ben said. "Though we may not all be able to go out at once. The boat is pretty small."

The man from the nearby table laughed.

"That should make it a nice snack for the monster."

Ben turned to the man. "Do you live near the lake?"

"Close, but not too close. I fish on it some." He stuck his hand out toward Ben. "I'm Art Northam. What are you planning to do with the monster if you find it?"

Ben shook the man's hand. "Film it. We have an online show, *Discover Cryptids*. This will be our first Canadian episode."

"And you take kids along?" the man said, disapproval clear in his voice.

"I don't just take them along," Ben said. "I depend on them. They're my crew."

"Well, you keep these boys safe," the man said. "I'd hate to hear of the monster making a snack of them."

"I don't want to be a snack," Tyler said. "We should get a really big, safe boat."

"The boat at the cabin will be fine," Sean insisted, frowning at Tyler. "We don't want a big boat that will scare away the creature."

"I don't know. I think I'm comfortable with scaring the monster a little," Tyler said. "Because it's already starting to scare me."

## chapter 4

# UNEXPECTED HELP

During lunch, Tyler declared poutine to be his new favorite food. That lasted until he tasted the pie, and it won the top spot. They were all slightly stuffed as they headed back outside for the walk to the cabin.

They didn't get far. The teenaged boy they'd seen earlier ran out the back door of the diner. "Wait up! Can I help?"

"Help with what?" Ben asked.

"Help you find the monster. I've lived here all my life. I could be a guide or something." The boy gave them a nervous grin and ran a hand through his hair before offering the same hand to Ben. "I'm Nathan Bruce." He pointed back toward the diner. "My mom owns this place."

Ben shook Nathan's hand. "We're always happy to have a good guide. Are you sure your mom can spare you?"

Nathan shoved his hands in his pockets. "With the monster wrecking boats at this end of the lake, we're hardly getting any business. I mostly hang out and watch Mom worry. I don't mind missing that."

They walked along a path that led away from the diner. "Do you think we'll be safe on the lake?" Tyler asked.

Nathan shrugged. "I don't know. Normally, I would say yes. But the monster has wrecked three boats. I've grown up hearing stories of the Turtle Lake Monster. This is the first time I've been afraid of it."

"The reports I read suggested the boat wrecks were from snags under the water," Sean said. "And reckless boat drivers."

"I know those people," Nathan insisted.

"They aren't reckless. They're good people. If you can find answers, I want to help."

"Do you know exactly where each of the attacks has taken place?" Ben asked.

Nathan nodded. "I can show you." He stopped and pointed ahead. "That's your cabin and the dock."

Ben looked between the cabin and the dock. "I have an idea. Tyler and Sean, you guys go check out the cabin. Make a list of things we need to pick up at the grocery." He handed over a key. "Gabe and I will go out for a quick look at the boat attack locations."

Tyler grinned. "You mean I get to skip being monster bait this time? Things are really looking up." He thumped Sean on the arm. "Let's go."

Sean frowned as he trotted after Tyler. "I do not understand why displays of friendliness with you always involve violence."

"Should I get the camera?" Gabe asked.

Ben paused, thinking about it. "Not this time. I just want to get a feel for the area."

"Yeah," Nathan said with a shrug. "All the spots I'm taking you just look like water."

They climbed into the motorboat with Ben in the back so he could steer. Gabe shrugged into one of the life vests that lay in the boat. He wrinkled his nose at the slight smell of mildew.

Nathan sat in the middle, so Ben could hear him clearly as he navigated. Gabe settled into the front.

Ben cranked the motor, and they puttered across the lake. Though it had been hot on the short walk from the diner, the breeze off the water felt almost chilly.

"Right about here," Nathan shouted. "This is where the Haskins hit something with their boat." He leaned over the side of the boat and peered into the water. "The boat sank fast. It's down there, but you can't see it."

"What about the Haskins? Did they see anything?" Ben asked.

Nathan shook his head. "Jake Haskins told me he and his dad were heading for their favorite fishing spot when something slammed into the boat. It caved in the whole side and dumped Jake and his dad into the water."

"But nothing attacked them in the water?" Ben asked.

"No. It's a good thing they had life vests on, because they had to swim to shore."

They visited the locations of the other two boat wrecks. All the wrecks were well away from shore. Also, they weren't close together.

Gabe thought that there was a pattern to the wrecks. If he could just figure it out! He didn't see any sign of debris in the water that the boats might have hit.

Nathan said, "All three boats were small, like this one."

Gabe wondered if the Turtle Lake Monster particularly hated little boats. "Maybe we should head back," he said nervously, glancing back at his brother. He hated to sound like Tyler, but he also didn't feel like a long swim in his clothes.

Ben didn't look worried, though he nodded. "We probably should. Leaving Sean and Tyler alone too long is just asking for trouble." Revving the motor, he turned the boat sharply. At the same moment, something struck the back corner of the boat, making it buck in the water.

"The monster!" Nathan yelled. "It's after us!"

## chapter 5

# THE CREATURE APPEARS!

Gabe had experience with monsters battering boats while he was in them. He hung on tightly and did not give in to the urge to lean over and look into the water. He was not going to be knocked overboard this time!

Ben circled the area slowly, watching the water. "Did you see anything?" he asked Gabe.

Gabe shook his head.

"Can we go back to shore now?" Nathan asked.

Ben grinned at him. "I thought you wanted to go monster hunting."

"Not in the water!" Nathan said.

"Whatever struck the boat seems to be gone now," Ben said. "If it's trying to sink boats, why

stop hitting us? We're obviously not sinking."

"Not sinking is a good thing," Nathan insisted.

"Good, but confusing. We'll come back out with a couple of cameras. I'd like one attached to the boat so it can watch the water the whole time." He turned the boat again. They headed back to the dock.

As soon as they reached the dock, Nathan sprung out. Once on the dock, he shoved his hands in his pockets and rocked on his toes nervously.

"We'll be going back out tomorrow," Ben said. "You coming?"

"No!" Nathan said. "Maybe. I don't know. I'll think about it."

"We'll be heading out about nine o'clock. Come join us if you want."

Nathan bobbed his head, "Maybe."

"See you," Gabe yelled as Nathan trotted away, back toward the grocery.

"What do you think of Nathan?" Ben asked when the teen was out of hearing.

"He's scared," Gabe said. "I was too. If you hadn't been turning when that thing hit, we could have been another wrecked boat."

"I think you're right." Ben clapped him on the back. "Let's go see what kind of trouble Tyler and Sean found while we were gone."

They found Sean sitting at the dining table in the cabin with his laptop open. Tyler lay on the futon in the living room area, reading comic books. He looked up when they came in. "There's no television and only one bedroom."

"Reading is better for you anyway," Ben said. "I'll sleep down here on the futon. You guys will take the beds in the loft."

He called the guys over and described the attack in the lake.

"Wow," Tyler said. "I almost wish I was there to see it."

"We didn't see anything," Ben said. "But something sure hit us."

"Let me guess," Tyler said. "We're going out tomorrow so it can try again."

"That's what makes us Monster Hunters," Gabe said, giving his friend a pat on the back. He wasn't completely comfortable with giving the monster another chance to try to drown them. But he knew they weren't likely to find the Turtle Lake Monster from the safety of shore.

Ben turned to Sean. "Did you find anything more on the attacks?"

"A little," Sean said. "No one has been seriously injured, though there have been bumps and bruises. Everyone wore life vests, so no drownings."

"So far," Tyler said.

Sean nodded. "So far. News coverage has been sparse. Most make fun of the idea of a lake monster."

"You said the boats might have hit trees, right?" Gabe asked.

"Snags," Sean said. "Dead trees that have fallen into the lake, then drifted with the current, hidden below the surface of the water. You'd be amazed at the damage that can do. Snags are more common in rivers. But reports say the lake is much lower this year because they've had so little rain." He shrugged. "Maybe that played a part."

"We didn't hit a snag," Gabe insisted. "Something attacked us. If Ben hadn't turned right then, we would have been sunk."

"It might have only seemed that way," Ben said. "We'll go back out tomorrow with the camera. We may learn more then."

Gabe nodded, but he was already certain. Something hit them on purpose.

Tyler finally started complaining about being hungry again, so Ben and Tyler left to get some

groceries and bring the van to the cabin. Sean turned back to his computer, and Gabe walked outside. Watching Sean research was boring. Gabe walked along the edge of the lake.

As soon as he was out of sight of the cabin, he stopped and looked around. Trees crowded close behind him, making it feel as though he were far from any other people. The huge lake was golden in the late afternoon sun. With the steady wind, the water moved constantly.

Gabe noticed the water was fairly shallow next to his feet. He could have waded in, if he'd felt like freezing. It was clear enough for Gabe to see the bottom was covered with piles of stones. Moving water had worked on the stones, smoothing away rough edges. They looked like the eggs of some giant creature, abandoned in the shallow water.

Again Gabe looked out over the surface of the lake. Suddenly, something burst from the

water, well away from shore. The creature had an elongated head that tapered down to a blunt snout. A fin of some sort stuck out from the back of the head and it had little ear fins. Bumps ran along the side of the creature's long neck. Gabe caught only the one quick look before it slammed back into the water.

Gabe watched the water until his eyes watered. He was afraid to blink in case he missed another appearance. When nothing burst from the water, he walked slowly back to the cabin, keeping his eyes on the lake as much as possible. When he walked right into a sapling, he tore his gaze away from the lake and paid more attention to the trail.

Gabe was glad to see Ben's van pulling up to the gravel pad next to the cabin. He ran to the van. Wait until the guys heard what he saw!

Tyler flung open the van door and ran toward Gabe.

"You won't believe it!" Gabe and Tyler yelled at the same time.

They both stopped talking and stared for a moment. Then Gabe said, "Believe what?"

"Someone tried to burn down the diner!" Tyler said.

Ben came around the van and nodded at what Tyler had said. "Whatever is going on around here, it's getting rougher."

42

## chapter 6

# ON THE
# LAKE

Later in the cabin, they talked about the fire for a while, though neither Ben nor Tyler had many details. "Are you sure the fire wasn't an accident?" Sean asked.

Ben shook his head, but Tyler said, "Nathan didn't think it was an accident. He was yelling that someone tried to kill his mom."

"Why would someone do that?" Gabe asked. "She seemed nice."

"That's a good question," Ben said.

"But the fire isn't really why we're here," Sean insisted. "We should focus on the monster."

That reminded Gabe of what he'd seen. He told them about it, even drawing a picture.

Tyler stared at the picture with wide eyes.

"That looks like the neck and head of a sea monster." He looked up at Gabe. "You saw a sea monster!"

"It is consistent with what people have reported seeing in the lake," Sean agreed. He pointed at the picture. "Is that an ear?"

"I'm not sure," Gabe admitted. "But it looked like one."

"Well, this is interesting," Ben said. "Maybe we'll catch sight of it again tomorrow. Right now, I'll try to put together some supper."

"Oh right," Tyler moaned as he grabbed his stomach. "We couldn't get food from the grocery. I'm going to starve!"

They didn't starve. Supper came from the few cans of food they had in the van. It's a good thing they all liked beans.

Afterward, they played a board game Tyler found in a closet. Then Ben borrowed Sean's computer to do a little research. Sean grumbled

about that for a while, then finally went to bed. Tyler and Gabe followed, leaving Ben downstairs peering into the glowing screen.

Once in bed, Gabe thought more about the creature he'd seen. Was that what rammed their boat? Would it try again?

The next day, Gabe was surprised to see Nathan trotting toward them as they headed out to the boat. Gabe waved. "How's your mom?"

"The doctors said the burn on her arm wasn't that bad," Nathan said. "So Mom came home last night. She says it hurts."

"That's too bad," Tyler said. "Your mom is nice."

Ben shifted the pack on his shoulder. "If you'd rather stay with your mom, I'd understand."

"The diner and grocery are closed. Mom told me she can rest better without me fussing over her." Nathan shrugged. "I think she wanted me to leave so she could talk to Mr. Northam."

"The man who was at the diner when we had lunch?" Gabe asked.

Nathan nodded. "Someone wants to buy the grocery and diner." He shrugged. "I don't know much about it. Mom says we're not selling, but Mr. Northam thinks we should."

"Anyone know how the fire started?" Ben asked.

"The fire marshal thinks Mom did it accidentally, or me. But we didn't. We don't lock the back door while the diner is open. Someone could have snuck in and started the fire"

"Maybe it has something to do with whoever wants to buy it," Tyler suggested.

Nathan shook his head. "That doesn't make sense. Why would someone burn something up if they wanted to buy it?"

Ben looked closely at Nathan. "Okay, let's get going. Sean's staying behind to do some research. I want to search this whole end of the

lake. Gabe saw something in the water last night, and I'd love to get some photos if we can."

Nathan looked at him curiously. "What did you see?"

Gabe pulled the drawing he'd made from his pocket. "This."

Nathan studied the picture. "Looks like a sea monster."

"That's what I thought," Tyler said.

Gabe folded the drawing back up with a shrug. "It's what I saw."

They reached the boat. Gabe attached one of the cameras to the edge of the boat as Ben passed out the life vests. "I found some interesting patterns in the attacks so I think we'll go over that area again," Ben said. "But first, I want to look at the shoreline."

"Why?" Gabe asked.

"Just gaining information," Ben said.

Once again Gabe took the spot at the front

of the boat. He pulled the second camera out of his backpack and began filming the water. He hoped to see the creature, but he also hoped they weren't rammed again.

As before, the water moved constantly in silvery ripples. The sun seemed hotter. Gabe could feel sweat trickle down his back under his T-shirt. He looked out at the banks of the lake. Small docks jutted out, but only a few had boats tied up to them.

"Are all these empty docks because of the attacks?" Gabe asked.

"Mostly," Nathan said. "Mr. Northam said some people have even sold their property."

"Mr. Northam seems very interested in property around the lake," said Ben.

"He's lived here a long time," Nathan said.

"Hey, guys!" Tyler pointed toward one of the docks. "Look! I think that man wants us."

On one of the docks, a man wildly waved his right arm in the air. His left arm hung in a sling. Ben turned the boat toward the dock. Soon they could hear the man shouting.

"Get out of the lake!" the man bellowed. "Get out now!"

## chapter 7

# THREATS!

Ben pulled up next to the small dock. "What's wrong?"

"Don't you know?" the man asked. "The monster attacks boats. It nearly killed me." He raised his arm in the sling. "It broke my arm!"

"We know about the monster," Ben said.

Gabe held up the camera. "We're collecting evidence."

The man gaped at them, then turned to Ben angrily. "The monster is dangerous!"

Tyler leaned forward and whispered loudly at Ben. "Maybe we should listen to this guy."

Ben simply said, "Tell us about your attack."

"The thing plowed right through my hull. I managed to get to shallow water, but my boat's

a total loss. I'm packing up and getting out of here."

"Did you see what attacked you?" Gabe asked.

The man nodded. "It was huge, with a long neck and big head."

Gabe pulled his drawing from his pocket. "Like this?"

The man seemed surprised by the drawing, but he nodded.

"Are you selling your house?" Ben asked.

The man gave him an odd look. "Who would buy it? The lake has a monster that attacks people."

"I heard some people sold their property," Ben said.

"Not me." The man shrugged. "I need to get back to packing." He pointed at Ben. "You should get these kids off the lake."

"Thanks for the advice," Ben said.

Once the man had walked away, Ben turned the boat back into the lake.

"I don't want to be on shore for this investigation," Gabe insisted.

"Don't worry," Ben said. "Where I go, you go. But I do have some questions." He stopped the boat and looked at Nathan. "Did you know that man?"

"Kind of," Nathan said. "That's Mr. Horton. I've seen him at the diner."

Ben nodded. "Do you know which properties have sold?"

"I know some of them," Nathan said.

"Can you show us?"

"Sure." Nathan directed Ben and the boat rumbled across the lake toward the diner. As the teenager pointed, a pattern quickly emerged. All of the sold properties were close to the diner.

"What do you think that means?" Gabe asked.

"I don't know," Ben said. "But it's interesting." He turned the boat away from shore and crisscrossed the lake for a couple of hours.

Gabe kept the camera slowly sweeping across the water the whole time. They were going to have a lot of video to go through, but it might show them something they were missing. So far, they hadn't seen anything all that interesting.

The sun moved directly overhead, pounding down on them. Tyler clutched his stomach. "I'm either sea sick or starving," he moaned.

"Fine," Ben said. "We should get out of the sun for a while anyway. We'll take a break and go out again in a few hours."

"I'll check on my mom," Nathan said.

"Do you live in one of the lake cabins? Can I drop you off?"

"We live in an apartment attached to the grocery, but you can't take the boat in there. The lake is really low behind the grocery and

diner, almost like a beach." He pointed toward a dock nearby. "You can drop me there. It isn't far to walk."

When they pulled up at the dock, Nathan jumped out. "I should probably hang out with my mom this afternoon. Are you going monster hunting tomorrow?"

"Maybe," Ben said. He gave Nathan his cell phone number so the teenager could call them. "Let me know if you or your mom need anything."

As Nathan trotted up the dock, Gabe watched his brother's face. "You think there's something going on here besides the monster, don't you."

"I think there might be," Ben said. Then he smiled at his brother. "And I'm a little worried about Nathan and his mom."

"Me too," Tyler said. "But I'm more worried about starving to death right here."

Ben rolled his eyes and revved the boat's

motor. In minutes they reached their own dock. As soon as they were in reach, Tyler jumped out to tie off the boat.

Gabe wished he'd seen the monster again. Even more, he wished he wasn't the only one who saw it. Sure, Mr. Horton told them he'd seen it, but something about the man felt wrong.

As soon as he finished tying off the boat, Tyler ran for the cabin.

"I guess the fridge is calling him," Ben said.

But Tyler didn't make it to the fridge. Instead they heard him yelling up ahead. Ben and Gabe broke into a run. They found Tyler pointing at the cabin's door. It was cracked open. Across the rough wood of the door, red, dripping letters read, "GET OFF THE LAKE!"

"Someone doesn't want us here," Gabe said.

"There's a bigger question," Ben responded as he shoved open the door and stomped inside. "Where's Sean?"

## chapter 8

# BREAK-IN!

As soon as they got inside, Ben bellowed Sean's name. Instantly, they heard a door open and Sean answer, "I'm here!"

Sean walked out of the small hallway to the bathroom, clutching his laptop. He glared at them. "It took you long enough! I was locked in the bathroom for one hour and sixteen minutes."

"Wow," Tyler said. "That beats my record!"

"I wasn't using it," Sean said as he walked by them and set his laptop on the kitchen table. "I was hiding. Well, actually, I was using it when someone broke in, but then I hid there. It's a good thing I always take my computer into the bathroom with me. Who knows what could have happened to it!"

Tyler rolled his eyes, then started picking up the things the intruder had thrown on the floor from the cupboards. He found an old package of crackers and tore into them while Ben quizzed Sean about the break-in.

"What do you know about the person who broke in?" Ben asked.

Sean thought for a moment.

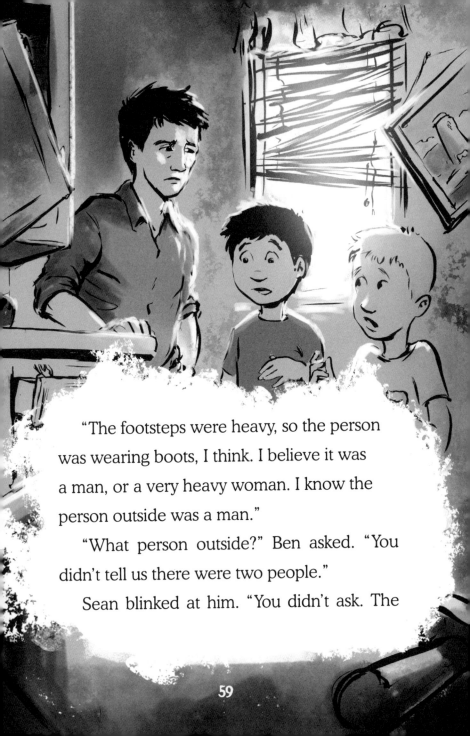

"The footsteps were heavy, so the person was wearing boots, I think. I believe it was a man, or a very heavy woman. I know the person outside was a man."

"What person outside?" Ben asked. "You didn't tell us there were two people."

Sean blinked at him. "You didn't ask. The

outside person yelled to the inside person at one point."

"What did he say?" Gabe asked.

"Let's go." Sean shrugged. "It wasn't particularly enlightening."

"Maybe not, but this is interesting," Ben said. "A monster might attack boats, but it doesn't write notes on cabin doors or trash kitchen cupboards. And a monster didn't set the fire at the diner."

"You think that fire was set on purpose?" Gabe asked.

"I'm starting to." Ben picked up one of the chairs knocked over by the intruder. "Let's clean up. Then we'll take the van and look for some place to buy lunch." He looked over at Tyler, who was holding an empty cracker wrapper. "I notice you didn't share."

Tyler wrinkled his nose. "They were pretty stale and bendy."

"Then why did you eat them?" Gabe asked.

"I'm starving."

Ben laughed and shook his head. "Well, help us pick up, and we'll go find you some real food before you pass away."

"While you clean, I'll start going through the camera footage you took today," Sean said as he settled down at the table.

Tyler rolled his eyes. "It's official. You'll do anything to get out of work."

Sean sniffed. "This is work. It's brain work."

"Well, try not to sprain anything," Tyler said.

Something about the word *sprain* tickled Gabe's memory. His brain was trying to tell him something, but he couldn't get it out. Finally he gave up. He'd remember when he remembered. There was no use driving himself nuts over it.

Gabe took a quick picture of the letters on the front door. Then he filled a bucket with hot water and soap suds.

"What's that for?" Tyler asked.

"I thought I'd scrub the note off the door." Gabe dropped a rag into the hot water, then hauled the heavy bucket to the front door. Just as he reached out to turn the handle, someone banged on the door, making Gabe jump. Hot soapy water sloshed against his legs.

He stood frozen for a moment, staring at the door.

"You can probably answer it," Ben said as he walked over. "I don't think intruders knock much."

Gabe opened the door and found Nathan standing with a bag in one hand. His mouth was open and he was pointing at the red letters. "Who did that?"

"That's what we'd like to know," Ben said. "It was there when we got back from the lake. I thought you were going to stay with your mom."

"I was. I am," Nathan stammered. He held

up the bag. "Mom said I should bring lunch over since the grocery still isn't open. She said to tell you she'll be open in the morning, for sure."

"Lunch!" Tyler bellowed. He practically snatched the bag from Nathan and peered inside. "Sandwiches and chips. We're saved."

"That's a little dramatic," Gabe said as his friend carried the bag to the table and dumped out the contents.

"Thanks," Ben said. "How much do I owe you for lunch?"

"Mom said it's on the house."

Ben pulled out his wallet and handed Nathan a handful of bills. "I insist. Tell your mom thanks for saving Tyler's life."

Nathan pointed at the writing on the door. "Why would someone do that?"

Ben frowned at the letters. "Because someone is driving people away from the lake."

Nathan's eyes widened. "Why?"

"I don't know yet," Ben answered. "And I don't know what it has to do with the Turtle Lake Monster." Ben looked at the teenager curiously. "You have any ideas about who might have done that?"

Nathan shook his head. "A lot of folks have left or are leaving, like Mr. Horton."

At that, Gabe suddenly yelped. He set down the heavy bucket of water and hurried across the room to Sean. "Didn't you tell me that none of the attacks resulted in serious injury?"

Sean nodded. "Bumps and bruises only, and soaking."

"How about a broken arm?" Gabe asked.

Sean shook his head. "Nothing that serious."

Gabe turned to his brother and Nathan at the door. "Then how did Mr. Horton get his broken arm?"

## chapter 9

# MONSTER
# OR NOT?

Sean turned to his computer, and Gabe waited while his friend typed and clicked for a minute. "None of the reports mention a broken arm."

"Maybe Mr. Horton didn't report it," Nathan said, stepping into the cabin and following Ben over to the table.

"Didn't report having his boat totaled and his arm broken?" Gabe asked.

Ben agreed. "To collect the insurance on the boat, he would have needed to report it."

Sean had turned back to the computer for more typing and clicking. "No reports mention anyone named Horton."

"I wonder why he wouldn't have reported

the attack," Gabe said. "It doesn't make sense."

"Maybe he didn't want to look like a kook," Tyler said.

"If he didn't want to look like a kook, why call us over and demand we get off the lake before the monster got us?" Gabe asked.

Nathan shrugged. "Maybe he thought that was his duty."

Ben leaned against the kitchen counter. "Did Mr. Horton suggest your mom sell the diner?"

Nathan shook his head. "He never mentioned selling. He wasn't exactly chatty when he came to the diner."

"Did you ever see him with strangers?" Ben asked.

Again Nathan shook his head. "He came in alone mostly, sometimes with Mr. Northam, but usually alone."

"He knows Mr. Northam?" Gabe asked.

"Most of us on the lake know each other."

Nathan's gaze traveled to the clock on the wall and he yelped. "I have to go. I told Mom I'd be right back."

As soon as he left, Gabe started scrubbing at the message on the front door. Ben walked over and leaned in the doorway. "You should come and have lunch."

"I will," Gabe said. "As soon as I clean up this mess."

"I'll try to keep Tyler from eating everything."

The paint on the door resisted scrubbing, but a spooky, pale pink warning seemed a lot less scary. Gabe was about ready to give up when Sean walked out.

"I have something to tell you," Sean said. "And show you."

Gabe scrubbed at the corner of the last letter, making the drippy part disappear entirely. "What?"

"You won't like it."

That got Gabe's attention. "Why not?"

Sean shrugged. "I think I know what you saw in the lake."

"The monster?" Gabe asked.

"The thing that seemed like a monster."

Gabe dropped the rag back into the bucket of pink water. "You better show me."

They walked into the kitchen. Ben and Tyler looked up from the table at the boys, but Sean didn't seem to notice. Gabe shrugged to show he didn't know what was going on either.

"I think this is what you saw." Sean turned the computer to Gabe. A large image of something jumping from the water filled the screen. Though it was some kind of fish, the front end looked a lot like what Gabe had seen on the lake. He felt his stomach sink. Was he fooled by a fish?

"What is that?" Tyler asked, his words muffled by the mouthful of sandwich. "It looks like your drawing."

"It's a sturgeon," Sean said. "The photo was taken in Florida. Sturgeons are bottom-feeders. I had no idea they ever jumped out of the water, but when water levels are low and it's very hot, sturgeons sometimes jump out of the water like this. They have even caused serious accidents by jumping into boats."

"That does look like what I saw," Gabe said glumly. "But do sturgeons ram boats?"

"Not according to anything I've read," Sean said.

Ben set the remains of his sandwich on the plate in front of him. He pointed at Sean's screen. "Even if that's what Gabe saw, it doesn't explain everything. Plus, Mr. Northam said no sturgeons have been found in the lake. I think we'd better go back out on the lake as soon as Gabe is done eating."

Gabe sat down at the table, but he didn't feel much like eating. He'd been so sure that he'd

seen the Turtle Lake Monster. "I'll wrap this up for later," he said. "I'm not hungry."

Ben nodded. "No problem. Come and help me grab a couple wet suits and oxygen tanks from the van. I think we're going to need to look below the surface for this mystery creature. The suits will let us stay in the cold water longer."

"Swim with a monster," Tyler said. "Why didn't I think of that?"

"Not you," Ben said. "Gabe and I. You're coming to watch the boat while we're diving."

"Aww," Tyler said, but he looked relieved.

Gabe headed out to the van. He wasn't sure how he felt about diving, but he knew he wanted the truth, even if it made him look silly.

Ben hauled open the van door and looked back at Gabe. "Don't feel bad. Anyone could have made that mistake."

*Then I wish anyone had*, Gabe thought. *Anyone else.*

## chapter 10

# HUNTING
# FOR ANSWERS

After Ben and Gabe pulled on wet suits, Gabe packed his sandwich and the camera into his backpack. He didn't want Ben to have to come back to shore if he suddenly got hungry.

Ben tapped Sean on top of the head. "Do you want to come with us?"

"Do I want to go sit in a boat in the hot sun?" Sean looked at Ben as if the answer should be obvious. "No."

"You're going to stay here alone?" Tyler asked. "After someone broke in earlier?"

"They already broke in," Sean answered. "Why come back? And I have all this video footage to go through."

"You're a braver man than I," Tyler said,

72

giving Sean a friendly thump on the back. Sean just waved them off, his eyes on the computer screen.

They headed out to the boat and piled in. Gabe slipped into his life vest. He'd take it off when it was time to dive, but he'd wear it until then. "Where are we going to dive?"

"Last night, I mapped out all the locations where the monster has attacked," Ben said. "I matched them to lake depth information Sean found. All the attacks follow a fairly straight line. The line matches a ridge below the surface of the lake. While we still have daylight, we're going to take a look at that same ridge."

They sped out to the ridge and were soon right on top of it. Ben turned off the motor. "We'll drift a little," he said. "But it shouldn't be too bad. Tyler, you watch for us."

"Should I be worried, sitting on top of the attack zone?" Tyler asked. "Because I am."

"I think you'll be all right," Ben said. "We'll check the area directly below us first. I have a theory. If my theory is correct, you should be fine."

"Then I hope your theory is correct," Tyler said. "Whatever it is."

Tyler and Gabe rolled into the water from opposite sides of the boat. Ben swam under and met Gabe on the other side. They rinsed their masks to help prevent fogging, then slipped them on. "What are we looking for?" Gabe asked.

"Anything weird," Ben said. "But especially any sign of heavy machinery."

Gabe nodded, though he wasn't sure what Ben expected to find under the water. He fit the mask tightly to his face, put the regulator in his mouth, and dove.

The water was murky, but Gabe and Ben each had bright lights clipped to their dive belts. They should help them see one another.

Gabe followed Ben as he swam along the ridge. Though he found some litter, Gabe saw no sign of heavy machinery. Several times, they swam to the surface and waved at Tyler. Each time, Tyler waved back and moved the boat closer to their position.

Finally, they spotted something huge in the murky water. For an instant, Gabe felt a jolt of panic. Was it the monster?

It wasn't. They had found a machine with what looked like a huge battering ram connected to springs. Gabe knew at once what it was, a boat basher.

Gabe took photos, swimming around the strange machine. The murky water kept them from seeing very far even with their lights. As a result, they didn't see the new diver until he grabbed Ben.

The diver was a big man in a dark wet suit. He and Ben struggled. Ben's regulator popped out of his mouth. The new diver could just hold Ben down until he drowned. Gabe had to do something.

He and Ben both always wore long bungee cords in a coil on their belts. You never knew when you'd need a good bungee. Gabe swam up to the struggling men and hooked one end of the cord to the attacker's scuba tank. The fighters never even paused.

Gabe pulled the cord, stretching it far enough to hook it to a metal loop on the huge battering ram. Then he simply pushed the lever on the machine. The battering ram rushed upward, dragging the diver with it.

After a couple of rides on the battering ram, the diver lost interest in fighting with anyone. Ben dragged him into their boat. Once aboard, Ben pulled the mask off the man.

"Mr. Northam!" Gabe said.

The next couple of hours were fairly exciting. The police arrived and arrested Mr. Northam and his partner, Mr. Horton. Each of the men quickly blamed the other for everything that had happened.

It turned out the boat basher had accidentally broken Mr. Horton's arm, leaving Mr. Northam to handle the big machine by himself. That's why it wasn't aimed well enough to sink the Monster Hunters' boat.

The two men were driving people away from the lake so they could buy enough property to build a resort. They wanted the diner property because it had the only beach section on that end of the lake.

"Well, we foiled the bad guys and won ourselves a great dinner," Tyler said when they finally got back to the cabin and found Nathan's mom had sent over hamburger soup and lots of hot, tasty poutine.

"I just wish I'd seen the real Turtle Lake Monster," Gabe said. "I'm glad we helped Nathan's mom, but we're the Monster Hunters. I thought I'd spotted a real cryptid."

"Actually, I believe you did," Sean said.

Gabe turned to stare at his friend. "You're the one who showed me pictures of jumping sturgeons. Why change your mind."

"I never change my mind," Sean said. "You did see a sturgeon the first time."

"What are you talking about?" Gabe asked. "I only saw the creature one time."

"With your eyes." Sean turned his laptop so Gabe could see a frozen image on the screen. "Your camera saw a little more."

The image was distant and not as clear as Gabe might have wished, but it definitely wasn't a sturgeon. The long-necked creature had a head that looked like a sea horse. As Sean clicked through the images frame by frame, the creature turned its head to look at the camera.

"The Turtle Lake Monster," Gabe said softly.

On the screen, the creature nodded at him, then dove back into the depths of the lake.